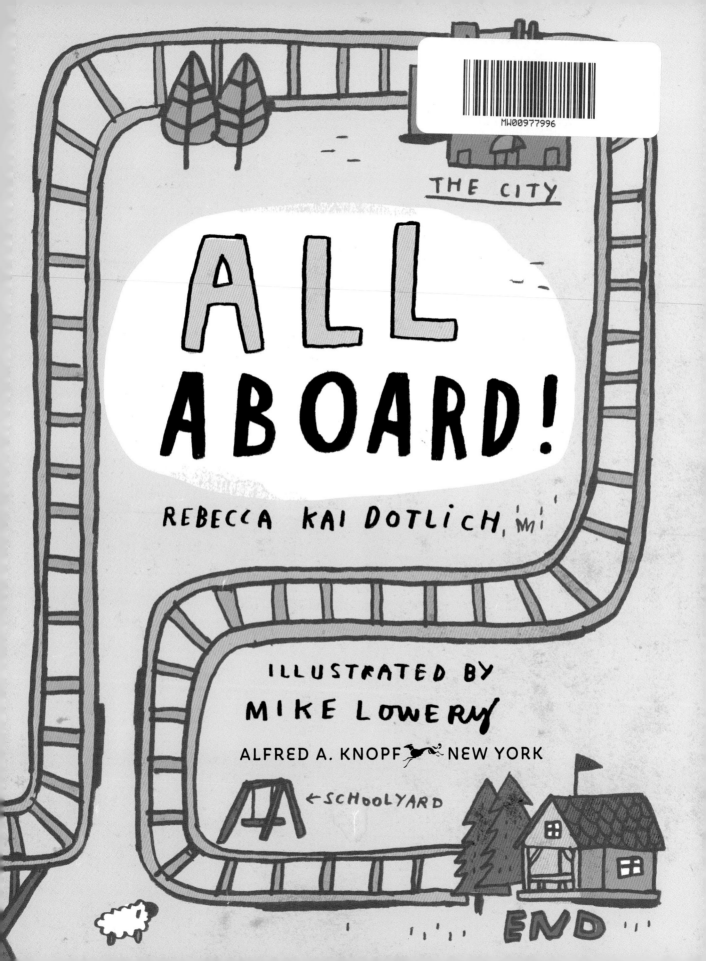

THE CITY

ALL ABOARD!

REBECCA KAI DOTLICH,

ILLUSTRATED BY

MIKE LOWERY

ALFRED A. KNOPF   NEW YORK

←SCHOOLYARD

END

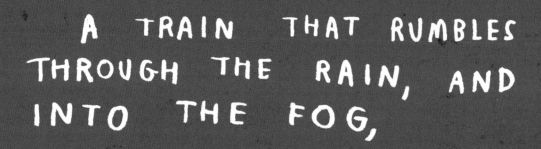

A TRAIN THAT RUMBLES THROUGH THE RAIN, AND INTO THE FOG,

AND UNDER THE MOON...

THERE'S PEOPLE AND PEOPLE AND PEOPLE AND... MORE!

A WARNING! CLANG, CLANG

AS THE TRAIN SCOOTS ALONG, A CLATTER-AND-CHUG

IN ITS RUMBLING SONG.

TRAINS CARRY BERRIES AND BEANS AND FISH,

AND SUGAR AND SYRUP,

TRAINS CAN HAUL TRACTORS

AND LUMBER

AND ROCK,

TRAINS WHISTLE
THROUGH PRAIRIES,
A LONG, STEEL SWEEP.
THROUGH **THUNDER**
AND **WIND**, THEY HAVE
SCHEDULES
TO KEEP.

WE SNAKE OUR WAY THROUGH A MOUNTAIN TOWN.
WHAT'S GOING ON? THE TRAIN'S SLOWING DOWN,
WITH A SQUEAK
AND A SCREEE

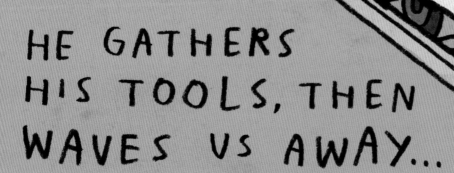

BY BRIDGES THAT SWAY
WITH A SPARKLE OF LIGHTS,

BY STONE WALLS AND SCHOOLYARDS,

CHUG, CHUG, CHUG,

WITH A SPIT AND A COUGH, WE PULL INTO THE STATION.

A BLAST OF A HORN!
A RUSH OF FRESH AIR...

STEP DOWN, LOOK AROUND—
SEE WHO'S
WAITING THERE!
PHEW!
WELCOME!
HELLO!
CAMP